My Family Is Forever

by
Nancy Carlson

VIKING

My Family Is Forever

To parents everywhere

with special thanks to Gail Fury

VIKING
Published by Penguin Group
Penguin Young Readers Group
345 Hudson Street, New York, New York 10014, U.S.A.
Penguin Books Ltd, 80 Strand, London WC2R 0RL, England
Penguin Books Australia Ltd, 250 Camberwell Road, Camberwell, Victoria 3124, Australia
Penguin Books Canada Ltd, 10 Alcorn Avenue, Toronto, Ontario, Canada M4V 3B2
Penguin Books (N.Z.) Ltd, 182-190 Wairau Road, Auckland 10, New Zealand

Published in 2004 by Viking, a division of Penguin Young Readers Group.

1 3 5 7 9 10 8 6 4 2

Copyright © Nancy Carlson, 2004
All rights reserved

LIBRARY OF CONGRESS CATALOGING-IN-PUBLICATION DATA
Carlson, Nancy L.
My family is forever / Nancy Carlson.
p. cm.
Summary: A young girl recounts how she came to be part of an adopted family.
ISBN 0-670-03650-1
[1. Adoption—Fiction. 2. Family—Fiction.] I. Title.
PZ7.C21665Myf 2004
[E]—dc22 2003012431

Manufactured in China
Set in Janson
Book designed by Kelley McIntyre

This is me. And this is my friend Jeffrey.

Jeffrey has his mom's red hair and his dad's big ears.

My family was formed by adoption, so I look just like . . . me! (And I'm pretty cute.)

Families are formed in different ways,

so they don't always look alike.

My mom and dad really wanted a child to love, and they looked forward to the day they would become parents.

So they asked an adoption counselor to help them find a child.

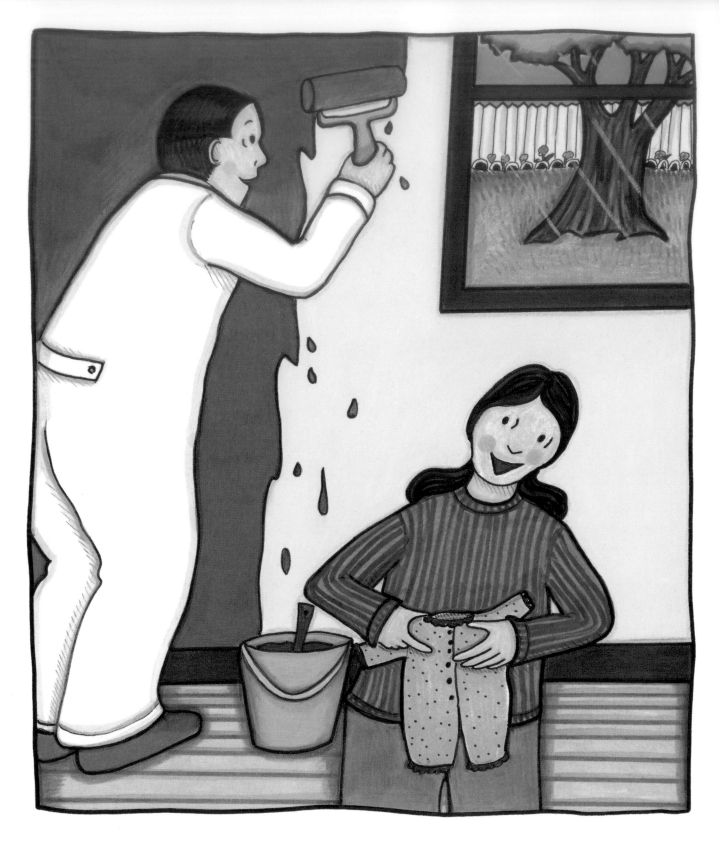

They had to wait and wait. But they were so excited about me that they found lots of ways to keep busy.

Then one day they got a call. It was time to go meet me!

Once I told Jeffrey I flew to my parents on a spaceship, just like a superhero.

Well, I *was* born far away, but my parents just took an airplane to come and get me.

And the moment they held me in their arms,
my parents knew we would be a family forever.

I've grown up a lot since then. These days, Dad
helps me with my homework . . .

and Mom plays catch with me.

I'm a good cook like my dad, and a wonderful dancer like my mom.

Besides my mom and dad, I have grandparents and aunts and uncles and cousins. Family parties are the best!

Sometimes I wonder about my birth parents.

Does my birth mother's hair stick up like mine?

Is my birth father a good reader like me?

One thing I know for sure is that they wanted me to
have a family to love—and I do!

Being a family means helping each other out.

We love each other in good times,

and we love each other even when things don't go
quite right.

And no matter where I go or what I do,

I'll always have my family by my side . . .

because families are forever!